1e

Henry and Mudge and the Tumbling Trip

The Twenty-Seventh Book of Their Adventures

by Cynthia Rylant
illustrated by Carolyn Bracken
in the style of Suçie Stevenson

Ready-to-Read

Simon Spotlight
New York London Toronto Sydney

THE HENRY AND MUDGE BOOKS

Simon Spotlight
An imprint of Simon & Schuster Children's Publishing Division
1230 Avenue of the Americas, New York, NY 10020
Text copyright © 2005 by Cynthia Rylant
Illustrations copyright © 2005 by Suçie Stevenson
Also available in a Simon & Schuster Books for Young Readers hardcover edition.
Designed by Lucy Ruth Cummins
The text of this book was set in 18-point Goudy.
The illustrations were rendered in pen-and-ink and watercolor.
Manufactured in the United States of America
First Aladdin Paperbacks edition October 2006
10
The Library of Congress has cataloged the hardcover edition as follows:
Rylant, Cynthia.
Henry and Mudge and the tumbling trip: the twenty-seventh book of their adventures / story by Cynthia Rylant; pictures by Suçie Stevenson.
p. cm.—(The Henry and Mudge books)
Summary: Henry, his parents, and his dog, Mudge, take a vacation out West, where they enjoy tumblewe
desert animals, souvenirs, and the wide open spaces.
[1. West (U.S.)—Fiction. 2. Vacations—Fiction. 3. Dogs—Fiction.] I. Stevenson, Suçie, ill. II. Title.
III. Series: Rylant, Cynthia. Henry and Mudge books.
PZ7.R982Heast 1999
[Fic.]—dc 21
98-20936
ISBN-13: 978-0-689-81180-7 (hc)
ISBN-10: 0-689-81180-2 (hc)
ISBN-13: 978-0-689-83452-3 (pbk)
ISBN-10: 0-689-83452-7 (pbk)
0512 LAK

Contents

Vacation!

When Henry and Henry's big dog, Mudge, went
into their kitchen one day, Henry's
parents were looking at a book.

The book was called *The Wild West.*

"Why are you reading about the West?" asked Henry.

"Because we are all going there," said Henry's mother. "On vacation."

7

"Wow!" said Henry. "Even Mudge?"

"Of course," said Henry's father.

"We need someone to round up all those cows."

Henry imagined Mudge rounding up cows.
Mudge would probably just kiss all of them.

"I can't wait to wear boots and cowboy hats," said Henry.

"Me too," said Henry's father.

"What can Mudge wear?" asked Henry.

They all looked at Mudge.

He was drooling on the floor.

"How about a bib?" asked Henry's dad.

12

Tumbling Tumbleweeds

Henry and Mudge and Henry's parents loaded
up their car and headed west.

Henry had lots of comic books and crossword puzzles to keep him busy on the trip.

Mudge just had an old shoe.
Mudge could keep busy for *years* with
an old shoe.

It was fun driving west.

The land got flatter.

The skies got bigger.

The people got taller.
(All those cowboy boots.)

"The West is *big*," Henry said at a rest stop. "Big enough even for Mudge," said Henry's father.

18

Mudge wagged his tail and knocked down
a parking sign.
"Well," said Henry's father, "maybe not."

At night the family checked into a motel.
It was called the Cowboy Inn.

The owner gave Henry a cowboy hat.
And he gave Mudge a bandanna.
"Wow!" said Henry. "Thanks!"

While Henry's father and mother rested in lawn chairs, Henry and Mudge chased tumbleweeds. They were everywhere and they were *fast*.

Henry pointed to one.
"Get it, Mudge!"
Mudge chased the tumbleweed.

He carried it back to Henry in his mouth.
"Good dog," said Henry.

Another tumbleweed tumbled by.
"Get it!"

Mudge chased that one.

Henry and Mudge chased tumbleweeds until dark.

When they were finished,
they had forty-two!
Henry's mother looked at
Mudge.
"I wish you could clean
the house as fast as you
can clean the West," she
told Mudge.

26

Mudge wagged.
He liked the West.
It had toys no one had to throw! 27

Home

The West was so much fun.
Henry and Mudge and Henry's parents went
to the desert. They saw strange cactus plants
and beautiful flowers.
The only thing Mudge saw was a lizard who
ran under a rock and wouldn't come out.

Henry and Mudge and Henry's parents went on long drives through canyons.

They saw rams on tall rock mountains.
"*Big* horns!" said Henry.

And the family stopped at souvenir shops.
Henry loved souvenirs.

He bought magnets and pencils.

He bought bandannas.

He bought a snow globe with a cowboy inside.

He bought Mudge some jerky.
"It's what all the cowboys chew, Mudge," said
Henry.

Mudge didn't care about chewing.
He swallowed the jerky in one gulp.

Mudge loved the West.

When their vacation was over,
Henry and Mudge and Henry's parents made the
long drive home.

The land got hillier.

The skies got smaller.

The people got shorter.

(No boots.)

But everything looked good.
Henry and Mudge were glad to be back home.

There were no tumbleweeds to chase.

No rams

or lizards.

But there were a million things just as fun right under Henry's bed.

Henry and Mudge had loved their
Wild West trip.

But they loved home best of all.